THE GREAT DETECTIVE
SHERLOCK HOLMES
— THE BLANCHED SOLDIER —

THE GREAT DETECTIVE
SHERLOCK HOLMES
—THE BLANCHED SOLDIER—

The Abandoned Well

At the English countryside of Bedfordshire, thick mist was ~~eerily~~ **overshadowing** the moon on this winter night at around 9 o'clock. The connecting road to the train station seemed even more spooky than usual under the dim moonlight fading in and out from behind the clouds.

A middle-aged man in travel wear was walking *briskly* on the road with a cane in his hand. He kept turning his head to look behind him, seemingly worried that he was being followed.

All of a sudden, a few footsteps sounded from behind him.

eerily (副) 詭異地　　overshadow(ing) (動) 遮蓋着　　spooky (形) 陰深恐怖的
briskly (副) 急速地

Startled by the noises, the middle-aged man stopped walking at once. He turned around to <u>assess</u> the situation. The road was quiet and empty. Suddenly, he could hear movement in the woods alongside the road, but it was too dark for him to see clearly.

Whether it was to **boost** his own courage or to scare off whomever that was hiding in the darkness, the middle-aged man shouted loudly, "Who is it? Why are you following me?"

But the **gloomy** forest was like a black hole. The darkness **sucked in** his voice completely without the slight bit of a returning echo.

assess (動) 評估　　boost (動) 提升、壯大　　gloomy (形) 陰森的
suck(ed) in (片語動) 吞沒了

Even though he could not see clearly with his eyes, years of experience as an investigator told the middle-aged man that there were definitely people in the woods, perhaps even three or four individuals. He could also sense that they had come with **ill intentions**, just like wolves hiding in the woods, waiting for the perfect timing to attack their prey.

Knowing that he was in a very dangerous situation, the middle-aged man decided to reverse his course. But after taking only a few hurrying steps, he could hear a low **growling** noise from behind. He quickly turned around only to find within the woods a pair of *glistening* blue eyes staring right at him.

ill intention(s) (名) 心懷不軌　prey (名) 獵物　growling (形) 低沉的咆哮
glistening (形) 閃閃發光的

"Oh no!" With no time to think twice, the middle-aged man *swiftly swung* **around** and ran. In that same *split second*, a **fierce** black dog burst out from the woods, barking and chasing after the middle-aged man.

The middle-aged man was so frightened that he ran with all his might. However, the dog was much faster in speed and the distance between them was shortened in no time. Just when the dog was about to reach the middle-aged man, the man threw his cane towards the dog with the pointy end aiming right at the dog. The man then made a sharp turn and ran into the woods.

The dog *agilely* *dodged* away from the flying cane then dashed into the woods, refusing to give up the *hot pursuit*.

swiftly（副）迅速地　swung (swing) around（片語動）轉身　split second（名）一剎那
fierce（形）兇猛的　pointy（形）尖的　agilely（副）靈活地　dodge(d)（動）閃避
hot pursuit（片語）窮追不捨

The middle-aged man kept running while panting **frantically**. "Aarrgghh!" A loud scream suddenly sounded from deep within the woods. The scream was followed by a **dull thud** then the middle-aged man had disappeared altogether.

"Woof, woof, woof, woof!" barked the fierce black dog.

"Over there!" said someone in the darkness.

Disorderly footsteps could be heard *shuffling* through the woods. A moment later, several human shadows showed up near the barking dog.

"Eh? Where is he?" asked one of the shadows.

"Woof, woof, woof, woof!" The fierce dog ran anxiously in small circles, as though it wished to convey a message to the shadows.

"Oh! Isn't there an **abandoned well** nearby? Could he have…" panicked one of the shadows as he thought aloud.

"The abandoned well!" said another shadow. "Rocky was running in small circles by that abandoned well!"

---

frantically (副) 拚命地　　dull thud (形＋名) 低沉的砰砰聲
shuffling (shuffle) (動) 拖拉的腳步　　abandoned well (形＋名) 荒廢的井

8

Apparently, Rocky was the name of the fierce black dog.

The shadows walked towards the spot where Rocky was still pacing in circles. Sure enough, there was a dark hole at that spot. "Woof, woof, woof, woof!" barked Rocky excitedly towards the hole, the same sort of bark that was meant to convey to his owner the location of a prey during a hunt.

"Could he have fallen down the well?" asked one shadow worriedly.

"Light up a **torch**," said a hoarse voice.

One of the shadows sparked a match then lit up a torch.

torch (名) 火把   hoarse (形) 沙啞的

9

As the shadow moved the torch above the well, all the other shadows stretched their necks to look down the well. This abandoned well was a dry well of about 20 feet deep. They could see the middle-aged man, who was running just a minute ago, now lying still at the bottom of the well.

"He fell and died?" asked one of the shadows apprehensively.

"Shall we help him up?" asked another shadow.

Everyone was quiet. No one offered an answer, as though they all had something to hide. The stillness hung in the air until one of the shadows could no longer withstand the silence, "Falling from such a height, he is probably dead."

stretch(ed) (動) 伸出、伸長   apprehensively (副) 戰戰兢兢地、憂慮地

"He fell down because he was careless. This wasn't our fault," said a trembling voice.

"Whether it's our fault or not, a man has died, and this will alarm the police, which means trouble for us," said the hoarse voice that spoke earlier.

Everyone was quiet again. Perhaps deep in their hearts, they knew that they had indirectly caused the death of this middle-aged man.

"Let's place the lid back on top of the well, so no one would ever fall down this well again," suggested the hoarse voice.

trembling (形) 顫抖的   lid (名) 蓋

The group gave each other a tacit look, because they knew the true intention behind those words. Together, they bent down to pick up the heavy lid that was lying beside the well and placed it on top of the well.

At this moment, the moon peeked from behind the misty clouds, shining a beam of pale moonlight through the bare tree branches, spotlighting the heavy lid that had now sealed off a life.

"Let's get out of here," urged a shaky voice.

As though those words were their cue, the shadows turned around all at once and walked off in hastened steps. After giving the lid a few sniffs, the black dog wagged its tale and followed its owner obediently out of the woods.

Just then, a few weak coughs sounded from the bottom of the well.

shaky (形) 發抖的   obediently (副) 順從地

12

A Friend Gone Missing

At 221B Baker Street, someone was knocking on the front door.

"So early in the morning and there is a visitor already," said Dr. Watson as he laid down the newspaper that he was reading and went to open the door.

The visitor was a tall man over six feet in height. His tanned complexion and his thin beard gave an impression that he was a strong and capable man.

tanned (形) 曬黑的　complexion (名) 膚色

Sherlock Holmes stood up, pointed at the sofa facing the window and said to the tall man, "Good morning. You've come here without an appointment so this must be a matter of urgency. Please take a seat."

"Yes, I have a **pressing** matter and I must see Mr. Sherlock Holmes at once," said the tall man politely as he handed his name card to Holmes and Watson.

After a quick glance at the name card, our great detective smiled and introduced himself to the tall man, "Mr. Dodd, I am Sherlock Holmes. This here is my good friend, Dr. Watson. He is a helpful partner in my investigative work."

"I…"

"South Africa. Did you just return from South Africa?" blurted Holmes before the tall man could utter another word.

Watson knew well that Holmes was showing off his observational skills again. This was a brilliant way to quickly gain confidence from clients, especially with clients who they had never met before.

pressing (形) 急切的　show(ing) off (片語動) 炫耀、賣弄

Sure enough, Dodd was impressed by Holmes's **intuition**. Struck by pleasant surprise, Dodd replied, "Why, yes."

"Were you a member of the **Imperial Yeomanry**?" pursued Holmes further.

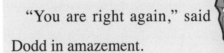

"You are right again," said Dodd in amazement.

"Middlesex Corps?"

"How did you know? That was the exact **regiment** I belonged to. Mr. Holmes, you must be a **wizard**."

It looks like Holmes has completely captivated this unexpected guest, thought the amused Watson.

---

intuition (名) 直覺　Imperial Yeomanry (名) 皇家義勇騎兵隊
regiment (名) 部隊、軍團　wizard (名) 變戲法的人

Holmes puffed a cloud of smoke from his pipe and casually disclosed how he figured out Dodd's identity, "First of all, you are an Englishman, but your complexion is tanned, a colour which cannot be achieved under the English sun. So I know you must've recently returned from a location with ample sunshine. Secondly, you've *tucked* your handkerchief up your sleeve. This is the habit of a soldier, which means you must've just left the military not too long ago. Thirdly, you keep your sideburns very short, indicating that you couldn't have been a soldier of the regular army. Fourthly, your haircut is the style of the cavalry, so your regiment must've been the cavalry. Lastly, your name card says you are a stockbroker and your office is on Throgmorton Street, which is the epicentre of security firms in London. Everyone knows that men from that area would only join the Middlesex Corps, and that corps had just recently returned from the war in South Africa. All I had to do was put those points together and the answer could not be simpler."

"Goodness me! You can see through everything," said the utterly impressed Dodd.

---

ample (形) 大量的、充足的　tuck(ed) (動) 塞進、放進　sideburns (名) 鬢角
cavalry (名) 騎兵　stockbroker (名) 股票經紀　epicentre (名) 集中地、中心

"Mr. Dodd, your words are too kind. But let's get back to business, shall we? So what is this matter that brought you to me today?" Now that Holmes had this new client wrapped around his little finger, Holmes ended the *idle chatter* and **cut to the chase**.

"Mr. Holmes, I would like to ask you to find someone for me," said Dodd.

 "Find someone? Who is this person?"

"He is a young man named Godfrey Emsworth. He is my good friend in the army."

 "Pray tell."

"This is what happened…" Dodd recounted his story in detail.

When I joined the army two years ago, young Godfrey was also enlisted to the same **squadron**. Godfrey was the only son of the retired **Colonel** Emsworth. The colonel was a very **stern** man. He was revered for his **valour** and **boldness** during the years he served in the military. His **illustrious** career had inspired Godfrey to

---

idle chatter (名) 閒聊　cut to the chase (習) 言歸正傳　pray tell (片語) 請說、洗耳恭聽
squadron (名) 中隊、戰隊　Colonel (名) 上校　stern (形) 嚴厲的、苛刻的
valour (名) 英勇　boldness (名) 膽識、膽量　illustrious (形) 輝煌的

join the volunteer army.

Godfrey was an outstanding soldier and everyone in our squadron was impressed by his fearlessness and quick wit. He and I fought shoulder to shoulder on the battlefield, facing all sorts of danger together. I almost died once when we were charging into battle. If Godfrey had not rescued me in the midst of **turmoil**, I would've lost my life for sure. As you can see, Godfrey and I are no ordinary friends. We have **gone through fire and water** together. We are blood brothers willing to die for each other. Our bond is absolutely unbreakable!

During the battle at Diamond Hill near Pretoria, Godfrey suffered a gunshot, but he was able to pull through. He wrote me two letters while he was recovering at the hospital. However, I have not received a word from him ever since.

After the war was over, I heard from other army mates that Godfrey had already returned to England. But if that were true, how come he hasn't written me a single letter? We are the best of mates, after all.

turmoil (名) 混亂   go(ne) through fire and water (片) 赴湯蹈火

Fortunately, I still have his home address so I wrote a letter to his father and asked him of Godfrey's *whereabouts*. As though I had tossed a message in a bottle to the sea, I never received a reply from the colonel. But I did not give up. I wrote to the colonel again. He replied this time, but only with a few lines saying Godfrey has gone away on a journey around the world and will not return to England for a year, basically implying that I should not waste any more time looking for Godfrey.

But that sounded *improbable* and *absurd* to me. Godfrey is a man who takes friendships and relationships seriously. It's not like him at all to leave the country for a year without saying goodbye to me first. So I began to *speculate* that something must've happened when he returned home after the war, otherwise all this **secrecy** wouldn't make any sense.

During our days together in the army, Godfrey told me that he and his father don't really get along too well. Godfrey said his father's sternness made it difficult to cultivate a close relationship with him. I **reckon** this could be a reason why the colonel is refusing to tell me where Godfrey is.

Since asking for information on Godfrey through writing letters to the colonel was ineffective, I wanted to pay a visit to Godfrey's home instead, thinking that I might be able to discover some sort of a lead over there. Remembering Godfrey once spoke of his closeness with his mother, I decided to write a letter to his mother. Rather than inquiring on the whereabouts of Godfrey, I changed my strategy and told his mother that I would like to share stories of Godfrey's experience at the war with her. His mother wrote back very quickly and invited me to their house to stay for a night.

secrecy (名) 保密、秘密　　cultivate (動) 建立、培養　　reckon (動) 認為

I accepted the invitation and went to their house a week ago. I arrived the Emsworth estate on the 2nd of February and spent two days there. What happened in those two days was so disconcerting that I'm now haunted by those memories forever!

The Austere Colonel

The sun was already setting when Dodd's train arrived the train station near Godfrey's home on the 2nd of February. This sparsely populated town in Bedfordshire was a picturesque small town that drew in many visitors every year between summer and autumn for hunting and sightseeing. Besides selling local farm produce, the town's main source of revenue mostly came from tourism.

sparsely (副) 稀少地   picturesque (形) 風光如畫的

Near the train station were a few small hotels. There were also some souvenir shops and pubs *catering to* visitors. However, business was far from booming on this cold winter day. Dodd was surprised to see no horse-drawn cabriolets parked outside the train station. He decided to take refuge from the cold at a nearby pub so he could ask the bartender the best way to go to Godfrey's home while warming his body with a glass of whisky.

The bartender was a big fellow. With a rather unfriendly look in his eyes, the bartender queried, "May I ask why do you want to go there?"

"I've been invited by Colonel Emsworth to stay the night at his home as a guest." Dodd **deliberately** only mentioned the colonel's name and not Godfrey's. Having experienced a war, he knew very well that the information one possessed could often be the *decisive factor* in winning a battle. His visit to Bedfordshire this time in search of Godfrey was, in a way, a battle of *pursuit*. He must gather as much information as

---

cater(ing) to (片語動) 迎合、服務   take refuge (片語) 避難、躲避
deliberately (副) 故意地   decisive factor (形＋名) 決定性因素、關鍵   pursuit (名) 追查

possible without exposing his purpose to strangers. So it was best for him not to talk too much.

"Oh, I see. You're a guest of the colonel's," said the bartender, looking more relaxed. "When you step out of the pub, turn right and you will see a road.  Walk down that road for about five miles and you will find the Emsworth estate."

"Thank you." Dodd thanked the bartender then tossed the rest of the whisky in the glass down his throat in one gulp. Just when Dodd was about to open the door to leave, the bartender called out to Dodd.

"It's getting dark outside. Remember to stay on the main road. Don't take any of the side roads and don't go into the woods alongside the road." The bartender further emphasised, "There are wild dogs in the woods and they attack unfamiliar faces."

"Thank you very much for the advice. I shall keep

that in mind." Dodd thanked the bartender again before leaving the pub.

Following the bartender's directions, Dodd turned right from the pub and went down the main road. After walking a mile or so, Dodd looked up to the sky and saw that it was starting to turn dark. He could still make out the shapes of the tall trees growing on both sides of the road. As it was **stark winter**, all the leaves had fallen and the trees were only left with bare branches.

"There are wild dogs in the woods and they attack unfamiliar faces."

The bartender's warning rang through Dodd's head again. Dodd **perked up** his ears and stayed alert as he kept walking, but there was only silence and stillness in the woods.

As Dodd moved on, he could see before him an old estate that was everything as grand as an estate should be. Surrounding a **majestic** mansion were vast green lawns. Also situated on the lawns but away from the mansion were several smaller houses. Encircling the vast lawns were the woods and bare trees.

stark winter (形+名) 嚴冬   perk(ed) up (片語動) 豎起(耳朵)
majestic (形) 雄偉的、莊嚴的

Dodd remembered Godfrey once told him, "My house is pretty big. It has more than twenty rooms. If we were to play hide-and-seek in my house, you probably wouldn't be able to find the person hiding even if you were to search for an entire day. Besides my parents, the only other people in the house is this old married couple who are our servants taking care of the whole house. Perhaps it's because there are so few people, the house always feels very empty and spooky, especially at night."

While thinking back on Godfrey's words, Dodd had reached the front door of the mansion.

An old *butler* of about sixty or seventy years of age came to greet him. With a gentle smile on his face, the old butler said, "Good evening, sir. You must be Mr. Dodd. My name is Ralph and I am the butler of this house. Mrs. Emsworth has been expecting you."

butler (名) 管家

The old butler was very polite and friendly. His **stiff**, **crooked** back was a sign of his lifelong **devotion** to his work and his utmost loyalty to the household. Dodd took an instant liking to this old butler right after meeting him. However, if Dodd were to be *pernickety*, he would say that Ralph's hoarse voice was rather uncomfortable to the ear.

Dodd followed Ralph through the mansion and into the living room. With *magnificent* oil paintings hanging on the walls and dark brown as the principal colour of the furniture, the living room felt **stuffy** and gloomy.

No wonder Godfrey thinks this house is spooky, thought Dodd as he sat down on the bulky sofa.

stiff (形) 僵硬的　crooked (形) 彎曲的　devotion (名) 鞠躬盡瘁、忠誠
pernickety (形) 吹毛求疵的、愛挑剔的　magnificent (形) 華麗的　stuffy (形) 悶熱的

Moments later, a tall and strong old man strode into the living room. The austerity in his face and his commanding presence clearly showed that he was a very serious man. Needless to say, this old man was Godfrey's father, Colonel Emsworth. Dodd realised right away that before him was not only a very tough man but also a very tough battle.

"Ralph, leave us be." After sending the butler away, the colonel sat down on the sofa across Dodd and asked in a rather hostile tone, "So what brings you here?"

Although Dodd was well prepared for this house visit, he was still taken aback by the colonel's blatantly unwelcoming manner. Dodd had not expected the colonel to be so directly **confrontational**, skipping all *niceties* and firing the first shot straightaway. But since the colonel was

---

strode (stride) (動) 大步走　austerity (名) 嚴肅　hostile (形) 懷敵意的、不友善的
blatantly (副) 明顯地、明目張膽地　confrontational (形) 咄咄逼人
niceties (nicety) (名) 禮節

29

his good friend's father, Dodd kept his cool and replied, "I've been invited by Mrs. Emsworth to come here and share with her stories of Godfrey on the battlefield…"

"That much I know," interrupted the colonel, waving his hand to cut off Dodd in midsentence, as though he was waving away an annoying fly. "You wrote in your letter that you are an army mate of Godfrey's. How would I know if you're telling the truth?"

"I have letters written to me from Godfrey," said Dodd as he reached into his pocket and pulled out an envelope.

"Let me see it," said the colonel. He reached over and *snatched* the envelope

snatch(ed) (動) 奪去

from Dodd's hand then began to read the letter.

Dodd could see the colonel's face ⇒*twitched*⇐ as he read the letter, but Dodd could not tell whether the colonel was touched by the sentiment of the letter or angered by the sheer existence of the letter. At the very least, the colonel was certain that letter was written by Godfrey, confirming Dodd really was Godfrey's army mate.

After reading the letter, the colonel handed them back to Dodd in a rough manner and said *bluntly*, "So what do you want?"

"Nothing. As I've told Mrs. Emsworth in my letter to her, I just

---

twitch(ed) (動) 抽動、抽搐   bluntly (副) 直言不諱地、不客氣地

want to talk to her about Godfrey…"

"No. I'm asking you what is your real purpose of coming here," interrupted the colonel again, coming straight to the point.

Dodd thought for a moment and decided not to *beat around the bush* any longer. Also coming straight to the point, Dodd said, "Your son, Godfrey, is a very good friend of mine. I haven't heard from him for a long time and I'd like to know where he is."

"Mr. Dodd, did I not make myself clear in my letter to you?" said the irritated colonel. "Godfrey felt exhausted physically and mentally after his experience in South Africa. He needed a break to rest his body and soul, so I made arrangements for him to take a trip around the world to help him forget the unpleasant ordeal."

"Is that so?" said Dodd. "May I ask when exactly did he depart for his journey? Also, can you tell me the name of the steamship on which he is travelling? I can send a letter to the steamer's next port. The letter should be able to reach Godfrey from there."

The old colonel had not expected Dodd to ask him this

beat around the bush (片語) 轉彎抹角   irritated (形) 生氣的、惱怒的
ordeal (名) 經歷、苦難   steamship (名) 輪船、郵輪

series of questions. In order to hold down his **glowering** frustration, the colonel *pursed* his lips and closed his eyes tightly. It was a good while before the colonel raised his head again and said crossly, "This concerns Godfrey's privacy. You can't just invade someone's privacy like that. Don't you have any manners, Mr. Dodd?"

glowering (形) 激怒的　　purse(d) (動) 噘着

"I apologise if I have offended you, sir, but Godfrey and I are very good friends. I believe that I have a right to know his whereabouts," said Dodd, trying his best not to raise his voice but he was beginning to lose his patience.

"I understand," said the old colonel. "But I must ask you to stop interfering. Every person and every family has their own secrets and ways of handling matters. Sometimes things are best left untold, as outsiders might not understand even when explained."

Just when Dodd was about to state his disagreement, an elegant old woman came into the living room. Needless to say, this old woman was Godfrey's mother. Before his wife had come close enough to hear him, the colonel said to Dodd in a stern tone, "My wife is very much interested in hearing about Godfrey's experience on the battlefield. You can tell her as much as you like, but please do not touch on the present and future status of Godfrey. I don't want you to break her heart. This is our family matter."

"And just like that, my first conversation with Colonel Emsworth came to a close," said Dodd to Holmes and Watson, coming back to present time. "Then I had dinner with the colonel and his wife. Godfrey's mother was a kind and *gracious* woman. She asked a lot about Godfrey's days in South Africa and she was happy to listen to all the stories. The colonel, on the other hand, held a grim face and didn't utter a word throughout dinner. As though the old couple made an agreement beforehand, Mrs. Emsworth did not mention one word about Godfrey's current whereabouts either."

"Hmmm...that sounds very odd indeed," said Holmes with his eyebrows *furrowed*. "Maybe something unspeakable really did happen to Godfrey."

gracious (形) 慈祥的、和藹的　　grim (形) 嚴肅的　　furrow(ed) (動) 皺起的

"After dinner, Ralph the old butler led me to one of the guestrooms. It was supposed to be just a simple good night rest. Who would've thought that something so frightening could happen," said Dodd with a sense of lingering **fear** in his voice.

Watson leaned his body forward in anticipation, as he knew that Dodd was about to reveal the most **intriguing** part of the story.

lingering fear (形＋名) 餘悸　　intriguing (形) 引人入勝的

The Blanched Face

The guestroom was **spacious**, dark and old-fashioned, furnished with only a bed, a desk and a chair. Facing the front lawn, the panorama of the front garden could be seen through the full-height **lattice glass door**. But since it was too dark outside, visibility was very low tonight.

Decided to **call it a day**, Dodd drew the curtain on one side of the glass door. Just when he was about to draw the curtain on the other side, Ralph came into the room with a bundle of firewood.

"Mr. Dodd, I've brought you more firewood, in case the wood in the fireplace burns up in the middle of the night," said Ralph as he placed the new firewood next to the fireplace.

---

spacious (形) 寬敞的　　furnish(ed) (動) 佈置　　panorama (名) 全景
lattice glass door (名) 格子玻璃門　　call it a day (習) 結束工作、今日到此為止

"It has been very cold these past couple of nights. The chill will definitely wake you up if the fireplace isn't kept burning the whole night to warm the room."

Ralph began to carefully add the new firewood into the fireplace. Satisfied with the crackling sounds of the burning firewood, Ralph turned around to Dodd and said with a gentle smile, "Mr. Dodd, while I was serving dinner earlier, I could not help but overhear the stories you were telling about young master Godfrey. He must've been an outstanding cavalry on the South African battlefields. My wife and I watched him grow up. He was like a son to us."

"I know. Godfrey has spoken to me about you and your wife," said Dodd. "Godfrey is such a brave soldier. He has even risked his life once to save my life."

Ralph's eyes shone

crackling (形) 劈啪的

with **enthusiasm** after hearing those words. He nodded his head repeatedly and said, "Oh yes, the young master must've been a brilliant soldier. You know, he was *dauntless* even as a lad. He had climbed every tree nearby, no matter the height. Nothing could stop the *feisty* lad. Oh, I miss him so much… He was such a good lad…"

Saddened by his own words, the old butler turned around to leave with a *dismal* look on his face. However, his last sentence had raised suspicion in Dodd. Dodd *grabbed hold of* the old butler's arm and asked, "Why did you say that just now? You said 'he was', you used the past tense. The way you spoke sounded like Godfrey has died!"

enthusiasm (名) 熱情　dauntless (形) 無畏的、勇敢的　lad (名) 小伙子
feisty (形) 精力充沛的　dismal (形) 悲傷絕望的　grab(bed) hold of (片語動) 抓住

Ralph was taken aback, but he assumed his **composure** at once and said, "What have I said? I was only **reminiscing** on the young master's days as a young boy."

"No!" said Dodd loudly as he pressed on. "That wasn't what you meant! Please tell me the truth. What happened to Godfrey?"

The old butler yanked off Dodd's hold and said, "Sir, I don't know what you're talking about. I am just a humble servant. It is not my position to say anything. If you have any questions, perhaps you should ask Colonel Emsworth."

After saying those words, Ralph quickly reached for the door to leave, but Dodd was not about to give up this opportunity to find the truth. Dodd swiftly **lunged** his body forward and blocked Ralph's way, asking a question that **pierced** right into his heart, "Ralph, is Godfrey dead?"

composure (名) 鎮靜　　reminiscing (reminisce) (動) 回憶、緬懷
lunge(d) (動) 撲向　　pierce(d) (動) 刺破、刺穿

The old butler staggered for a moment. He had not expected Dodd to ask such a thing, but he seemed unperturbed by the piercing question. Ralph shook his head and said plaintively, "You want to know if Godfrey is dead? How I wish he really were dead…"

"What?" Dodd could not believe his own ears.

"I wish he really were dead!" The old butler suddenly raised his head and said with bitter frustration, "He is better off dead!"

After saying those words, Ralph pushed off Dodd and stepped out of the room, his trembling footsteps disappearing into the darkness of the corridor.

Dodd did not chase after Ralph. He knew that the old butler would not reveal anything more even if he were to pursue. Letting out a sigh, Dodd closed the room door and sat down on the chair beside the curtain. Although his mind was in chaos, his military training had equipped him with the ability to collect his calm quickly.

"I wish he really were dead!" Ralph's shocking words kept spinning around and echoing in Dodd's mind.

---

stagger(ed) (動) 震驚　unperturbed (形) 不擔憂的、平靜的
plaintively (副) 哀愁地、傷感地

If Godfrey were already dead, Ralph wouldn't say 'I wish he really were dead'. But those words that he was muttering to himself earlier, 'Oh, I miss him so much... He was such a good lad...' That could only mean Godfrey is no longer a good lad. Could Godfrey have committed a **heinous** crime that brings shame to his parents? A **deed** so horrible that breaks the heart of the old butler who watched him grow up? pondered Dodd.

Dodd began to theorise in his mind, *That must be it.*

heinous (形) 令人髮指的、十惡不赦的　　deed (名) 行為　　ponder(ed) (動) 沉思

Godfrey is a brave chap but he can also be reckless*.*
Perhaps he did something really bad and the colonel
tossed him out of his own home. In order to save the
family name and keep the scandal a secret, they've come
up with a lie about Godfrey's trip around the world
without revealing exactly where Godfrey is.

The thought of that theory made Dodd feel
disheartened. For one second, he even wondered
whether he should carry on with his investigation, but
his determination returned right away. As Godfrey's
good friend, he believed that Godfrey needed his help
now more than ever. No matter what Godfrey had done,
Dodd was fixed on finding the truth.

At that moment, the corner of Dodd's eye noticed
something moving near the glass door on the side where
the curtain was not drawn. **Out of reflex**, Dodd turned his
head towards that direction and was stunned to see a man's
face pressed against the glass, and the man's face was as
pale as a ghost! The blanched face was peeking into the
house sneakily as though he was looking for something.

---

reckless (形) 魯莽   toss(ed) out (片話動) 驅逐   disheartened (形) 沮喪的、洩氣的
out of reflex (片語) 本能反應地

43

Before Dodd could even collect his senses, the blanched face turned towards Dodd and the two men caught each other's eyes. Those were a pair of familiar eyes. Dodd had shared his thoughts and feelings while looking into those melancholic eyes many times during the difficult nights in South Africa. It was how they pulled each other through those long, unbearable nights.

Godfrey! That has to be Godfrey! Those are the eyes of a living man! I can see sadness, self-pity and regret in his eyes! Godfrey is not dead!

Dodd quickly collected himself from the initial shock and immediately lunged towards the glass door, but the blanched-faced man's reaction was even quicker, swiftly swinging his body around and ran off. Dodd tried to turn the knob of the glass door, but he was in such frenzy that it took him a few seconds before he could finally open the glass door and run out of the house. The blanched-faced man was consumed by the darkness of the night by then, but Dodd could still hear his running footsteps. Dodd ran towards the direction of the footstep noises for several dozen yards, then a loud bang

melancholic (形) 憂鬱的　　frenzy (名) 瘋狂　　consume(d) (動) 被吞噬

sounded and there were no more footstep noises. Everything returned to silence once again.

Dodd stopped running and turned his head to look at his surroundings. He could see several small houses scattered in front of him, but none of the houses were lit. He speculated that the bang he heard a moment ago must have been the sound of a shutting door, but it was too dark to see exactly which house the blanched-faced man went into. As Dodd wondered whether he should go around knocking on the door of each house, he could hear a low growl approaching him. Steadying his eyes, Dodd could see a fierce black dog blocking his way before him.

Dodd could tell from the posture of the dog that if he were to take one more

scatter(ed) (動) 散佈、分散　shutting (形) 關閉的

step forward, the dog would launch
an attack on him. In order not to
§provoke§ the dog, Dodd decided to
cautiously take a few steps backwards
then slowly walk back to his room.

Unable to fall asleep, the image of
that blanched face kept appearing
in Dodd's head all through the
night. Even though the complexion
was as white as paste, Dodd was very certain that the
blanched face was his good friend, Godfrey. But what
had happened to Godfrey that made his skin shed all
colours? Why did Godfrey run when their eyes met
each other? Dodd *tossed and turned* in his bed but still
could not think of any answers that made sense. Just
when the sun was beginning to rise, Dodd finally came
up with an idea to use his time wisely while he was
there for a deeper investigation.

During breakfast, Godfrey's mother eagerly suggested
a few nearby sightseeing spots to Dodd.

provoke (動) 激怒、挑釁   toss(ed) and turn(ed) (習) 輾轉反側、翻來覆去

"Thank you very much for your suggestions. Now that I'm here, I'd like to spend more time looking around this beautiful town. Would you be so kind as to allow me to stay one more night please?" asked Dodd.

The colonel's face stiffened , clearly not liking the idea. Just when he was about to turn down Dodd's request, Mrs. Emsworth said cheerfully, "Of course. We seldom have any guests here. Extending your stay would only make this big house more lively."

Seeing that his wife had already welcomed Dodd to spend more time with them, Colonel Emsworth had no choice but to nod in agreement.

stiffen(ed) (動) 變得生硬、變得拘謹

After breakfast was finished, Dodd thanked the Emsworths for their **hospitality** and pretended to head out for some sightseeing. However, once he stepped out of the mansion, he quietly turned towards the lawn where the smaller houses were. Dodd knew that the noise of the shutting door he heard last night probably came from one of those houses.

Just when Dodd was nearing the largest of the small houses, a middle-aged man of short **stature** came out from that house. He was wearing a **dapper** suit with a tie knotted neatly around the collar. He did not look like a servant at all.

The man seemed surprised when he saw Dodd approaching the house, "Excuse me, sir, are you a guest of the colonel's?"

"Yes, I am a good friend of his son's, Godfrey." Dodd deliberately mentioned Godfrey's name to see the middle-aged gentleman's reaction.

"Oh..." The middle-aged gentleman seemed slightly **taken aback**, but did not say anything more.

hospitality (名) 殷勤款待、熱情好客   stature (名) 身形、身材
dapper (形) 衣冠楚楚的   take(n) aback (片語動) 嚇一跳、出乎意料

49

"But the timing of my visit isn't right. It's a shame that Godfrey has gone travelling, otherwise he would've been so happy to see me come all the way to visit him," said Dodd, further testing the water.

"Yes... a shame indeed," said the middle-aged gentleman awkwardly. "Perhaps you can come back again when he returns from his trip." As though he had something to hide, the middle-aged gentleman walked away hastily after saying those words.

Pretending to take a leisurely stroll, Dodd slowly circled around the house that the middle-aged gentleman came out from. Every window of the house was drawn with thick curtains. Dodd could not see the interior of the house at all.

test(ing) the water (習) 試探　　awkwardly (副) 局促不安地、尷尬地　　hastily (副) 匆忙地
stroll (名) 散步

Dodd did not stop and stand outside the house since he did not wish to draw attention. He just casually walked on by. However, just when he was about to walk away from the house, Dodd could see faintly that the middle-aged gentleman had been watching him all this time from a distance in the dark woods. Dodd then left the estate and visited the nearby sightseeing spots suggested by Mrs. Emsworth, but his mind was too preoccupied with the investigation that he was in no mood to enjoy the beautiful sceneries.

After dinner, Dodd went back to his room and waited for the night to fall. He waited until 10 o'clock in the evening before he quietly opened the glass door and slipped outside. After the encounter with the fierce dog last night, Dodd brought with him a stick of firewood tonight, in case he needed to fend for himself.

The moon was shining bright tonight. And since Dodd had walked to the house earlier during the day, reaching the house tonight was much easier. It was also his luck that the fierce dog from last night had not shown up tonight. Dodd scurried to the front of a window at the small house. The window was drawn with thick curtains the same way it was during daytime, but Dodd

fend (動) 保衛   scurried (scurry) (動) 匆匆跑到

could see **a crack** of light shining from the gap between the curtains. Peeking through the gap, Dodd could see the living room of the house. All the lights were lit and the fireplace was burning.

The short gentleman that he met earlier in the day was reading some sort of periodical. There was another man sitting on a chair in the living room with his back to the window. This man seemed to be staring at the fireplace. Even though Dodd could not see this man's face, just one look of his back and Dodd knew for certain that this man was Godfrey. Dodd could recognise the shape of those shoulders and arms anywhere. After all, Dodd and Godfrey had gone through fire and water

a crack (名) 一條縫   periodical (名) 期刊

together, fighting side by side during the war.
Everything about Godfrey was unforgettable to Dodd.

Just when Dodd was deliberating what he should do
next, a large hand suddenly
landed on his shoulder. Dodd
turned around in surprise, only

to find a very angry Colonel Emsworth glaring at him.

"Come with me!" growled the colonel in a low voice. Apparently, the colonel did not want to disturb the people inside the small house.

Dodd had no choice but to follow the colonel to a large tree nearby. The colonel pulled out a sheet of paper with times written on it and said to Dodd in a commanding tone, "This is the train's timetable for tomorrow morning. There is a train leaving for London at 8:30 in the morning. You will take that train. I have arranged for a carriage to wait at the front door tomorrow morning at 8 o'clock."

"I was just…"

"I don't want to hear it." The colonel cut off Dodd in midsentence before continuing. "Your behaviour is utterly **loathsome**. On one hand, you claim to be a good friend of Godfrey's. On the other hand, you **lurk around** and overstep **boundaries**, looking for God knows what. I never want to speak with you again. And I never want to see your face ever again!"

loathsome (形) 令人討厭　lurk around (片語動) 鬼鬼祟祟行動
boundaries (boundary) (名) 界限

After listening to the colonel's *berating* words, Dodd also **laid out his cards on the table** without reservations , "But I saw Godfrey! I don't know why you are hiding Godfrey from the world, but I'm telling you right now, sir, you might be Godfrey's father but I am Godfrey's good friend! I will never give up until I learn the truth!"

With anger blazing in his eyes, the colonel stared down at Dodd furiously as though he was about to give Dodd a punch. However, after a few deep breaths, he was able to control his anger and walked off without saying another word.

Dodd could not quiet his nerves after his encounter with the colonel. Turning his head towards the direction

berating (形) 責備的　　laid (lay) out his cards on the table (片語動) 攤牌、和盤托出
without reservations (片語) 毫無保留地、毫不猶豫地

of the small house, Dodd considered going back for another look. Just then he noticed a pair of glistening blue eyes staring right at him from behind a tree. Dodd knew that those eyes must belong to the fierce black dog from last night. Instead of risking an attack, Dodd had no choice but to retreat back to his room.

The next morning, Dodd left the Emsworth estate with a heavy heart and headed back to London on the 8:30 a.m. train…

The Missing Private Investigator

"So my investigation came to stop right there," said the **dejected** Dodd.

Holmes pondered for a moment then asked, "Are you certain that the man you saw outside the glass door was Godfrey?"

"I am very sure. He was so close to the glass door that his entire face was **practically** pressing against the glass. Even though it was dark outside, the lighting inside the room was bright enough for me to see his face and eyes clearly."

dejected (形) 沮喪的、失望的　　practically (副) 幾乎、差不多

"If the room were that bright, that meant he could see the entire room clearly too. So why did he need to press his face against the glass door?" asked Holmes **sceptically**.

"That probably had to do with where I was sitting," explained Dodd. "The right side curtain was drawn and I was sitting on the right of that drawn curtain. That was pretty much a **blind spot** from the glass door. If he didn't press his face against the glass door, he probably wouldn't be able to see me."

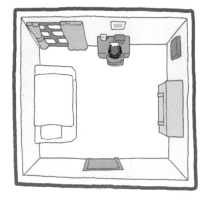

"I see," nodded Holmes. "And that's why you're so sure that man was Godfrey?"

"Yes," replied Dodd. "Even though his complexion was distinctly different, I could still recognise his eyes, his shape and his back."

"You said that his complexion was as white as a

sceptically (副) 懷疑地　blind spot (名) 盲點

ghost. Was the whiteness even?" Holmes was known for his attention to every detail.

Dodd thought for a moment then said, "The whiteness wasn't very even. They were **patches** of white with **cracks** on the patches, similar to the **peeling** white paint on a weathered wall. I couldn't help but gasp in horror when I first saw his face."

"Hmmmm..." Holmes crossed his elbows and lowered his head. After a moment of thinking, he suddenly raised his head and asked, "What about that middle-aged man you came across outside the wooden house? You said he didn't look like a servant to you?"

Watson was accustomed to Holmes's **unpredictable** questioning manner, but the rapid shift of topics

patch(es) (名) 一片片、一塊塊　crack(s) (名) 裂紋　peeling (形) 剝落的
weathered (形) 風化的、褪色的　unpredictable (形) 出其不意的

seemed all too abrupt, for Dodd.

"Erm... That man...?" Dodd stumbled for a bit before replying, "Do you mean that short gentleman? He didn't seem like a servant at all with the way he dressed and spoke."

"You said you peeked through the curtain gaps and saw him reading some sort of periodical. Did you see which newspaper was it?"

"Which newspaper was he reading? Is that important?" uttered Dodd, finding this question rather odd. Watson also thought this question was somewhat **trivial**, but knowing his old partner, Holmes must have noticed something worth exploring.

"Very important," said Holmes matter-of-factly.

"I'm sorry but I didn't pay attention. My

---

abrupt (形) 突然的　　stumble(d) (動) 遲疑　　trivial (形) 微不足道的、瑣碎的

mind was not focused on gathering such details at that time."

"No need to apologise. That's very normal. But do you remember if the periodical was large or small?"

"Do you mean the size of the paper?" Dodd thought for a moment then replied, "I think it was small, like the size of the weeklies."

"Excellent," said Holmes with a satisfied  grin.

Holmes then switched the topic once again,

grin (名) 露齒笑

"Besides the old servant couple, were there other servants coming in and out of that estate?"

"No. Whether it was indoors or outdoors, the old couple was the only servants I saw on the estate."

"Have you seen the old butler bringing food to that wooden house?" Holmes switched to another topic yet again.

"I'm not sure, but around sunset on the second day of my visit, I did see the old butler carry a basket covered with a piece of cloth to that wooden house," said Dodd. "Come to think of it, he might be bringing dinner to Godfrey."

"No need to jump to conclusions just yet," said Holmes. "You said you spoke with the bartender at a pub near the train station. Did you speak with any other local residents after that?"

"No," said Dodd as he shook his head. "But

I did stroll around the area near the train station when I went out for sightseeing. Maybe because it's wintertime and there weren't other tourists, I kept having this feeling that all the townspeople were watching my every move. The bartender was definitely watching me. Even the middle-aged man sweeping the ground outside the hotel and the souvenir shop lady both kept sneaking peeks at me."

Holmes furrowed his eyebrows and said, "Hmmm... Perhaps the situation is more complicated than expected."

"Actually..." blurted Dodd hesitantly.

Holmes and Watson turned to each other. They could

blurt(ed) (動) 突然說   hesitantly (副) 猶豫地

sense there was more information that this sudden new client had yet to **divulge**.

"Mr. Dodd, if you want to find out the truth, you must tell me everything that you know. Withholding information would only **hinder** my investigation," reminded Holmes **sternly**.

"I understand." Dodd made up his mind and said, "Actually, before coming here, I've hired another private investigator to help me with the case."

"What?" Holmes and Watson were both taken aback.

"The next day after I returned to London from Godfrey's home, that's the 5th of February, I went to see a private investigator named

---

divulge (動) 透露　hinder (動) 妨礙　sternly (副) 嚴厲地

Harp. I was told that Mr. Harp is an expert in finding missing persons."

"Harp? I know him. He is indeed an expert in finding missing persons, mainly helping parents find their runaway children or helping **moneylenders** locate their **debtors**," said Holmes. "If you've already **commissioned** Harp to find your friend, why have you come here to see me today?"

"Because... Mr. Harp has gone missing."

"What?" *gasped* Holmes and Watson *in surprise*.

"After listening to my story, Mr. Harp quickly agreed to take my case. He even said he would begin his investigation right away," said Dodd. "We were supposed to meet again on the 8th of February, upon which he would update me on his progress."

"He didn't come to the meeting?" asked Holmes.

"No," replied Dodd. "I went to his office on the 8th as planned, but his secretary told me he hadn't returned yet. She said I should wait another day. But when I went back again the next day, which was yesterday,

---

moneylender(s) (名) 放債者   debtor(s) (名) 欠債者   commission(ed) (動) 委託
gasp(ed) in surprise (習) 驚歎

Harp was still not at his office. His secretary said she had not heard a word from him and she was starting to feel worried."

"So Harp has gone missing ever since he went to visit the Emsworths. How many days has it been?" asked Holmes.

"According to his secretary, he rode a train to Bedfordshire on the 6th of February. This means he has been missing for four days already, counting today," said the concerned Dodd.

"This is not good. Not good at all," uttered Holmes worryingly, which was unusual of him. "If he were fine and only needed to stay in Bedfordshire for a few more days, he would've sent a telegram to his secretary. Something must've happened to him."

"I didn't expect searching for Godfrey would be such a dangerous task. This is all my fault." Dodd could not help but blame himself.

"But what exactly has happened to Mr. Harp?" interjected Watson.

"It's hard to say. Maybe Harp figured out the truth behind Godfrey's disappearance, then someone decided to ~~get rid of~~ Harp in order to bury the secret," said Holmes.

"Get rid of?" asked Dodd in trepidation. "Do you mean...?"

Holmes only nodded his head without saying a word, but from the grim expression on Holmes's face, Dodd and Watson both knew that "get rid of" must bear the same meaning as "kill". After all, a dead man does not talk.

get rid of (片語動) 除掉　　trepidation (名) 驚恐不安、惴惴不安

Bumping into Scotland Yard's Detective Duo

Since it was a matter of life and death, Holmes, Watson and Dodd wasted no time and headed towards Bedfordshire straightaway.

While on the train, Watson asked, "Two men are missing now. One is Godfrey, Mr. Dodd's army mate. The other one is Harp, the private investigator. Who should we look for first?"

"Good question," said Holmes. "I've given this some thought. I think we should focus on finding Godfrey first. Only after we find Godfrey can we hope to find some leads on Harp."

"Why is that?" asked Dodd.

"The reason is simple. You've seen Godfrey twice already. If your eyes hadn't *defied* you, this means

defied (defy) (動) 違抗

Godfrey is still alive. Finding someone who is still alive is much easier than finding someone who might already be dead."

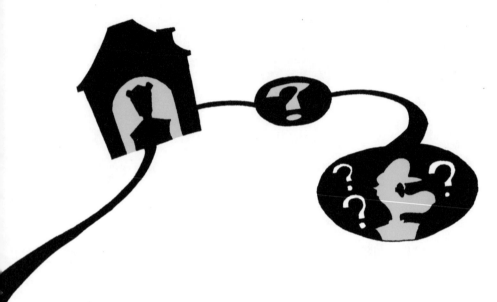

Watson nodded, "That sounds reasonable. If Godfrey were still alive, there is a good chance he is holed up somewhere near the Emsworth's mansion. But if Harp were killed as a means to silence him, then he is probably now buried in a very hidden location. Finding a dead body is not easy at all."

"And how should we go about finding Harp after we

find Godfrey?" asked Dodd.

"Once we find Godfrey, we will know the secret behind his hiding away from the world," said Holmes confidently. "This secret must be related to Harp's missing. Someone must be very determined to keep this secret concealed forever, so determined that Harp must be silenced by death."

"Oh God, this is terrible! What if it were Godfrey or his father who killed Harp? What should we do then?" fretted Dodd.

"Don't be so worried. We are only talking about **hypothesis**. Who knows? Maybe Harp is lucky enough to be alive and out of harm's way?"

However, Watson knew that his old partner was only saying that to Dodd to calm him down. The truth of the matter was that the odds of Harp still being alive were probably slim to none.

Two hours later, their train arrived at the train station nearest Godfrey's home. Just when Holmes was about to ask Dodd to lead the way after they stepped off the

determined (形) 堅決的　conceal(ed) (動) 隱藏　fret(ted) (動) 苦惱、發愁
hypothesis (名) 假設　odds (名) 可能性　slim to none (習) 微乎其微、近乎零

71

train, Holmes saw two familiar figures also getting off the train from another passenger carriage.

"Aren't they Gorilla and Fox from Scotland Yard?" Watson had also noticed the two men.

Dodd was taken aback and asked, "Scotland Yard detectives? Are you serious? Does this mean…?"

"Perhaps they've also come here to investigate Harp's missing," said Holmes, speaking Dodd's mind. "Harp's secretary must've reported his missing to the police."

"Should we go say hello?" Watson asked his old partner.

Holmes thought for a second then said, "Let's not disturb them before they notice us. It would only complicate matters."

Watson understood Holmes's concern. The last thing they needed was for the **foolhardy** Scotland Yard's detective duo to mess up their investigation.

In a rather *dubious* manner, Gorilla and Fox stepped out of the train station then walked down a nearby road after taking a look at the paper in their hands.

foolhardy (形) 魯莽的、有勇無謀的　　dubious (形) 可疑的

"Where are they heading?" muttered Holmes.

"Godfrey's home is down that road," said Dodd.

"This is not good. If the duo were to reach the estate before we do, they may sound the alarm," said Holmes with his eyebrows furrowed.

"What should we do then?" asked Watson.

"Let's follow behind them for now and **play by ear** ."

The three men kept a distance behind the Scotland Yard duo as they headed towards Godfrey's home.

Shortly after they started walking down the main road, Watson asked Holmes, "They seemed different than usual when I first saw them at the train station. This feeling is only getting stronger as we keep following

play by ear (片語) 見機行事、隨機應變

them, but I can't **pinpoint** exactly what is different about them. Are you having the same feeling?"

"Yes, I noticed it right away as soon as I saw them. Are you not seeing it?" said Holmes.

"So what's different about them?" asked Watson.

"Watson, you've joined me in so many cases before. Are you still not able to make out such a simple

pinpoint (動) 確定

observation?" said Holmes with an **impatient** sigh. "I'll tell you about it later. You just keep observing them. It's not a big deal anyway."

However, what Holmes considered to be "not a big deal" would later turn out to be the key to finding Harp's whereabouts!

(Readers, can you see how the Scotland Yard duo is different from their **usual selves** ?)

---

impatient (形) 不耐煩的   usual selves (self) (片語) 老樣子、一貫作風

The Reunion

As Holmes, Watson and Dodd quietly followed behind Gorilla and Fox, the group reached the part of the road that was beside the woods. Gorilla and Fox continued walking for about another mile before taking a halt.

The duo whispered something to each other then *strode* eagerly into the woods.

"What should we do now? Should we keep following them?" asked Watson.

"No," said Holmes decidedly. "Let's stick to our plan and go find Godfrey first, since he is the key to solving all the mysteries."

Following our great detective's

strode (stride) (動) 大步行走

instructions, Dodd quickened his steps and led Holmes and Watson towards the Emsworths' estate.

After about two more miles of walking, the three men reached the front of the main large mansion. Just then, Ralph the old butler approached them while holding a leash that was tied to a fierce black dog.

Dodd recognised the dog right away and whispered to Holmes, "This was the fierce dog that blocked my way that night."

"Woof, woof, woof!" warned the black dog at the three men with its loud barks.

"Rocky, back down!" commanded the old butler at the dog. "They are our guests." Ralph's hoarse voice carried *an air of authority*.

The black dog lowered its head and let out a few whimpers before lying down on its belly, as though it was apologising for its bad behaviour.

"What an **obedient** dog," said Holmes as he knelt down next to the black dog and gave its head a few playful, rough strokes. Watson knew well that Holmes had this special ability to make friends with dogs right away, no matter how aggressive the dogs might seem.

an air of authority (名) 威嚴的語氣　　obedient (形) 服從的、聽話的

As though speaking with some sort of <u>underlying implication</u>, the old butler said, "Rocky is a very obedient dog, but he could also be ferocious, especially when he sees strangers."

"I must say that I got to know that capability first-hand. This dog can be very ferocious indeed." Dodd then switched the subject and asked Ralph, "Pardon me, but is the colonel at home? We would like to see him. Can you please pass the message?"

The old butler felt a bit unsure about these three uninvited visitors. He hesitated for a moment, wondering if he should deny Dodd's request, but at last decided to consent, "The colonel is home. Please wait here for a moment." Ralph slowly turned his **curved back** and walked into the main mansion after saying those words.

Holmes waited until Ralph was **out of earshot** before whispering to Watson and Dodd, "His glove carries an odour of sterilising solution."

"Really? I hadn't noticed," said Watson.

underlying implication (名) 言外之意、隱藏的意思
ferocious (形) 兇惡的　curved back (名) 駝背、彎曲的背部
out of earshot (習) 聽不到的範圍　sterilising solution (名) 消毒藥水

"When I knelt down to touch the dog, I deliberately leaned close to his hand that was near the dog's head to take a sniff."

"You knelt down to touch the dog because you needed to get close to his glove?" asked Dodd in amazement.

"Yes," said Holmes. "The fact that he was wearing gloves **concurred** with my initial theory, so I wanted to confirm."

"Initial theory? What theory?" asked Dodd.

Just when Holmes was about to reply Dodd, Colonel

concur(red) (動) 脗合、一致

Emsworth came to the front door. He turned to Dodd and shouted angrily, "Didn't I tell you not to come here anymore? Why are you here again? Leave now! I don't ever want to see you again!"

"I am not leaving!" said Dodd, refusing to back down. "Not until I see Godfrey and he explains to me in person why he is hiding."

With his **veins popping** furiously on his forehead, the colonel turned around and yelled, "Ralph! Call the police right now! Tell them there are **intruders** *trespassing* on my property!"

"Sir, if I may introduce myself," said Holmes as he leaned forward and handed his name card to the colonel. "I am a private detective from London and..."

"I don't care who you are! All of you, get off my estate right now!" Before Holmes could even finish

vein(s) pop(ping) (名＋動) 青筋暴起   intruder(s) (名) 不速之客
trespass(ing) (動) 擅自進入

81

his self-introduction, the colonel had already snatched the name card from Holmes's hand, torn it in half then tossed it *irritably* onto the ground.

"Ralph! Call the police! Call the police right now!" demanded the colonel when the old butler reappeared at the front door.

"You won't call the police," said Holmes all of a sudden.

Taken aback, the old colonel **growled**, "Why wouldn't I call the police?"

"Because of your son."

"What do you mean?"

"You don't want to expose your son's secret."

"Secret...? We don't have any secrets!"

"Is that so? By all means, please call the police then."

"You...!" The old colonel was so **infuriated** that he

irritably (副) 暴躁地   growl(ed) (動) 怒吼   infuriated (形) 憤怒的、生氣的

was lost for words.

Holmes slowly pulled a sheet of paper out of his notebook. He wrote a single word on the paper and handed it to the colonel.

The old colonel's face was filled with apprehension when he took the notepaper from Holmes's hand. After just one look at the written word, the colonel felt weak at the knees and caved in *like a deflated ball*.

The sight of the defeated colonel **bewildered** both Watson and Dodd. Exactly what did Holmes write on that sheet of paper that could make the raging colonel lose his will to battle?

apprehension (名) 憂慮、擔心   cave(d) in (片語動) 屈服、妥協
like a deflated ball (片語) 像洩了氣的皮球   bewilder(ed) (動) 困惑

It took the old colonel a great deal of effort to steady his footing. He asked in a frail voice, "You... How did you know?"

"I'm sorry, but this is my expertise," said Holmes. "I am very skilled at uncovering secrets."

"I give up. If you really wish to see Godfrey, then go see him." With his sturdy fortress breached by Holmes's one written word, the disheartened colonel continued wistfully, "I knew this day would come eventually. I give up. You can go see him." Tears welling in his eyes, Colonel Emsworth gestured towards Ralph, who was staggered by

frail (形) 虛弱的　expertise (名) 專長　sturdy fortress (形＋名) 堅固的堡壘
disheartened (形) 沮喪的　wistfully (副) 傷感地　stagger(ed) (動) 嚇呆的、震驚的

the colonel's sudden change in demeanour.

The old butler slowly came back to his senses then turned **clumsily** to the three men and said, "Sirs, this way please." Leading the way in trembling steps, Ralph took the men to the small wooden houses on the other side of the vast lawn. Rocky the black dog followed loyally beside its master with its tail **wagging** calmly.

After reaching the particular house that Dodd had mentioned earlier, Ralph knocked on the front door gently several times and said, "Dr. Kent, Master Godfrey's friends are here to see him."

Dr. Kent? There is a doctor on this estate? wondered Watson.

Before Watson had time to think it through, Holmes whispered in his ear, "Just as I had expected, there is a **peer** of your profession in this place."

Just as he had expected? Watson was greatly surprised by Holmes's words. Is it possible that Holmes knew all along there's a doctor here? How did he know?

The men waited outside the front door for a while but there was no response from the house, so Ralph decided

demeanour (名) 態度　clumsily (副) 笨拙地、不靈活地　wag(ging) (動) 搖擺
peer (名) 同行

85

to turn the doorknob and open the door himself. As soon as they stepped into the house, they could see a man standing in the living room with his back towards them, staring at the burning fireplace.

"Godfrey!" exclaimed Dodd, recognising this man straightaway. "I've come to see you."

As the man slowly turned around, his unevenly blanched face was exposed to all eyes.

"Oh God! Is that…?" uttered the **astounded** Watson. In that instant, the name of a disease flashed across his mind, a disease so dreadful that the mere mentioning of the name could bring immense fear in people!

Watson could also tell from the contour of Godfrey's face that Godfrey must have been a very handsome young man before he got sick. His good looks in

astounded (形) 震驚的　　mere (形) 僅僅的、只不過的　　immense (形) 極大的
contour (名) 輪廓

the past must have brought on extensive mental and emotional agony on top of the physical discomfort he was suffering. The extreme change could often result in more unbearable misery.

Godfrey was shocked for a moment to see his best mate standing before him. He quickly gathered his senses and said, "You are here at last, Dodd. When I saw you that night, I knew you would come back for sure. I know you too well. You are not a man who would give up easily when it comes to pursuing the truth."

"So why did you avoid me?" Dodd took a large step forward, extending his arm towards Godfrey, wishing to shake the hand of his best mate that he had not seen for a long time. But instead of taking Dodd's hand, Godfrey raised his arm to stop Dodd, "Please don't touch me! I've been infected with a terrible disease. I don't want to pass it onto you."

agony (名) 痛苦

"I'm not scared."

"I know, because you are my best mate," said Godfrey. "I'm very happy that you've come looking for me, but I'm not who I was any longer. I cannot show my face in public. I can only live out the rest of my life in hiding.

"Why? Why do you need to do that?"

"It's a long story." Godfrey let out a deep sigh before continuing, "Remember the battle at Diamond Hill? In the midst of turmoil, Anderson, Simpson and I got separated from the rest of the cavalry and were soon surrounded by enemy troops. We decided to fight our way out. Both Anderson and Simpson died from enemy gunfire. I also took a bullet in my right arm, but luckily my horse's strong fighting spirit pulled me through. My horse was shot many times in the hail of bullets, but it kept *sprinting* until we broke through the enemy line. My brave **stallion** kept running for several more miles before it finally keeled over in a forest.

"Oh my God…" Dodd shared Godfrey's sadness as he listened to Godfrey's story.

"I fell off the horse and passed out on the ground. I

sprint(ing) (動) 全速跑、奮力跑　stallion (名) 馬　keel(ed) over (片語動) 倒下

must've been out for a long while, because by the time I was awakened by the icy raindrops, the night had already fallen. I used my left hand to press onto the gun wound on my right arm, got up on my feet and noticed a large house not too far away. As you know, the temperature difference between day and night in South Africa was pretty extreme. The nights could be cold as winter. I knew that in my weakened physical condition, I probably wouldn't be able to survive if I were to stay outdoors through the night, so I decided to bear the pain and walk to the house. As soon as I stepped into the house, I could see rows of empty beds inside and it felt like a safe place to me. By then, I was just too *exhausted* and my knees gave in. I collapsed onto one of the beds and fell asleep." Godfrey paused for a moment before he *grimaced* and shook his head, "But I had no idea at that time that was only the beginning of an *eternal* nightmare!"

---

exhausted (形) 筋疲力盡的   grimace(d) (動) 臉部扭曲   eternal (形) 永無休止的

The Beginning
of a Nightmare

Sunrays were already beaming brightly onto my bed
by the time I finally woke up the next morning. As soon
as I opened my eyes, I was greatly taken aback because
a group of ugly faces were surrounding my bed. They
stared at me curiously as they whispered in each other's
ears. I could not understand what they were saying, but
I was pretty sure that they were all talking about me.

Before I could think of what to do next, a very short
but strong man pushed his way through all those people
and came to my bedside. He began shouting at me
angrily and even tried to pull me off the bed.

When I tried to *yank* his grip off my arm, my wound was *agitated* and I started screaming in pain. Instead of helping me, those spectators around my bed *sneered* and cheered in excitement.

Just then, an old gentleman walked into the room. Unlike the others, he had a normal face and he seemed to be a man of authority. He let out a commanding shout and the group of spectators *dispersed* right away.

The old gentleman came to my bedside and said to me in English, "Young man, what brought you here?"

Soon after the old gentleman asked the question, he noticed my wound before I gave my reply, "Oh my God! You're wounded, and pretty badly too."

I nodded, "Yes, I was shot in the shoulder."

The old gentleman gave me a *once-over* then asked, "From the look of your

yank (動) 猛拉　agitate(d) (動) 觸碰、觸動　sneer(ed) (動) 嘲笑、譏諷
disperse(d) (動) 散開　once-over (名) 上下打量、掃視

uniform, you must belong to the cavalry of the British army. I heard that there was a fierce battle over at Diamond Hill yesterday. Were you…?"

I nodded in silence.

"You might've survived the perils of a fierce battle, but if I were you, I would not have slept in this bed," said the old gentleman as he pointed at my bed.

I thought he meant I should not have occupied someone's bed without asking for permission first, so I explained my circumstances, "I apologise for my intrusion, but I was wounded and was just too exhausted last night. Since I didn't see anyone here, I just plopped down and fell asleep."

"No, you're misunderstanding me," said the old gentleman as he shook his head. "What I mean is that this bed is more

peril(s) (名) 危險   intrusion (名) 擅闖   plop(ped) down (片語動) 倒下

dangerous than the battlefield."

I did not understand what he was saying, so I just looked at him **blankly**.

"These beds are for patients suffering from an **infectious disease**, and that includes the bed you're in right now." The old man took a pause before uttering the name of that particular disease. I was stunned speechless as soon as I heard the name, as though my head was struck by lightning.

I found out later that hospital specialised in taking in patients who needed to be **isolated**. The hospital was worried that the ongoing battle might spread to their area, so they *evacuated* everyone to another location the night before I went in. They came back after the fighting was over. That old gentleman was the hospital's director. He was a very kind man. Not only did he treat my wounds, he also made the arrangements to send me to a hospital in Cape Town.

"Don't you understand? I have an **incurable** disease," said Godfrey bitterly after recounting his horrible

---

blankly (副) 茫然地、毫無表情地　　infectious disease (形＋名) 傳染病

isolate(d) (動) 隔離　　evacuate(d) (動) 撤離　　incurable (形) 無法治癒的、藥石無靈的

experience. "I became very sick soon after I came home."

Dodd was lost for words. His eyes were **reddened** with tears. He finally understood why his best mate went into hiding. He knew well that if Godfrey's sickness were made public, no one would want to associate with the Emsworth family anymore. People in general were so fearful of infectious diseases that they would **"shun"** those who had **contracted** infectious diseases. If not handled well, Godfrey could be locked up in an isolation hospital and lose his freedom forever.

Holmes, who had been listening in silence all this time, finally began to speak. After a brief introduction of himself, Holmes asked Godfrey, "Where is that doctor who is with you?"

"Oh, do you mean Dr. Kent? He went out early this morning," replied Godfrey.

Upon hearing the exchange of words, Watson could no longer contain his curiosity, "Holmes, how did you know there is a doctor here?"

"Mr. Dodd told me."

redden(ed) (動) 變得通紅　　shun (動) 排斥、避開　　contract(ed) (動) 感染

"Me?" asked the baffled Dodd.

"Yes," said Holmes. "You mentioned that you met a middle-aged gentleman outside this house. You even said you saw him reading a periodical that was about the same size as the weeklies when you peeked into the house."

"You figured out he was a doctor just from those information?" asked Dodd.

"Of course not, but I came to the conclusion after considering all the other information that you've also given me," said Holmes as he began to explain his analysis.

1 Dodd said he saw Godfrey's blanched face on the other side of the glass door and the *discolouration* looked uneven. This means that Godfrey is sick and whatever that he is suffering from is causing changes in the colour of his skin.

2 The Emsworths are determined to keep Godfrey away from other people. Even Godfrey himself does not want to meet his best mate. This means whatever Godfrey is suffering from is no ordinary illness, perhaps

discolouration (名) 變色、褪色

96

an infectious disease so horrible that the mentioning of the name is enough to scare the devil out of people. Moreover, Godfrey is an only child, yet he is not living in the main mansion but is instead dwelling in a small wooden house that's separated by a distance from the main mansion. This point further supports the infectious disease theory, because their living arrangement is basically the same as patient isolation. Also, having the old butler bring meals to this small house regularly further indicates that Godfrey is living in isolation. Otherwise, why is Godfrey not eating his meals with his parents? The fact that I could smell an odour of sterilising solution on the old butler's glove earlier proves my theory is correct.

3 When Dodd asked Ralph whether Godfrey had died or not, Ralph's reply was "I wish he really were dead! He is better off dead!" Ralph blurted out those words in bitter frustration, which could only mean Godfrey's illness is no ordinary disease. Not

scare the devil out of (習) 嚇得魂不附體

only is the patient suffering in agony, the people around him are also feeling incredibly sad and helpless. Only an incurable disease can bring about such grim hopelessness.

④ If Godfrey really had contracted an incurable disease, the colonel would definitely hire a medical professional to treat and look after his son day and night since the family certainly has the financial means to afford private homecare. Dodd said the middle-aged gentleman he met outside the house did not look or speak like a servant, yet he was staying in the same house with Godfrey. This suggests that he is probably a doctor. The fact that the periodical he was reading was about the same size as the weeklies further proves this point, because the medical journal is about the same size as the weeklies. More importantly, the law requires a patient suffering from infectious diseases to hire a private doctor to look after the patient when *opting* for homecare instead of hospitalisation.

Holmes turned his head to look at everyone inside the house before he concluded, "It is from all the above observations and deductions that I am certain there is a doctor staying here at all times. Since there is no one else living on

opt(ing) (動) 選擇

this estate besides the Emsworths, Ralph and his wife, that middle-aged gentleman must be the doctor."

"Mr. Holmes, you are brilliant. You saw through everything. Your deduction is precisely accurate," said Godfrey.

Dodd thought for a moment then asked, "So what is this infectious disease?" Dodd's eyes moved from Holmes to Godfrey, as though he was not sure to whom he should direct the question.

Holmes did not offer a reply but looked over to Godfrey instead. Only then did Watson realise that Godfrey had not mentioned the name of his illness while he was **recounting** his experience. Holmes also did not mention the disease name when explaining his deduction process. It was obvious that Holmes had deliberately omitted mentioning the name. He knew well that the name was not just a medical term to Godfrey; it was also a **traumatic** experience that he was still going through. Godfrey must be feeling unbearably painful every time the name was mentioned.

"No need to ask. The answer is right here," said a

recount(ing) (動) 敘述　　traumatic (形) 痛苦難忘的、造成精神創傷的

voice from behind.

Everyone in the room turned around and found the old

colonel standing by the door, holding up a
piece of notepaper in his hand.

*Isn't that the note that Holmes handed
to the old colonel earlier?* thought
Watson.

Dodd walked
towards Colonel Emsworth
and took the notepaper.
After just one look at the
writing, Dodd was shocked stiff and his
face went completely pale. Holmes gave a *consoling*
pat on Dodd's shoulder before taking the notepaper

consoling (形) 安慰的

from Dodd and handed it to Watson, "Watson, this is the disease."

Watson took the notepaper. There was only one single word written on it, but it was enough for Watson to finally understand why the old colonel gave up his resistance and broke down, because the word was "Leprosy", the horrible contagious disease feared by all. It was also exactly what Watson had suspected when Watson first saw Godfrey.

But how did Holmes figure out Godfrey is suffering from leprosy just from Dodd's description? Watson thought for a moment then suddenly remembered an article he had read recently in the medical journal about how leprosy was spreading near Cape Town in South Africa. *The changes to Godfrey's face matches the early symptoms of a leper. Being a naturally curious man, Holmes always enjoys reading my medical journal subscriptions. Holmes must have read that article too.*

Watson's speculation was spot on. Holmes's line of reasoning was precisely as such.

"Colonel Emsworth, has Godfrey been seen by other

leprosy (名) 麻風病　contagious (形) 傳染性的、會傳染的　leper (名) 麻風病人
speculation (動) 猜測

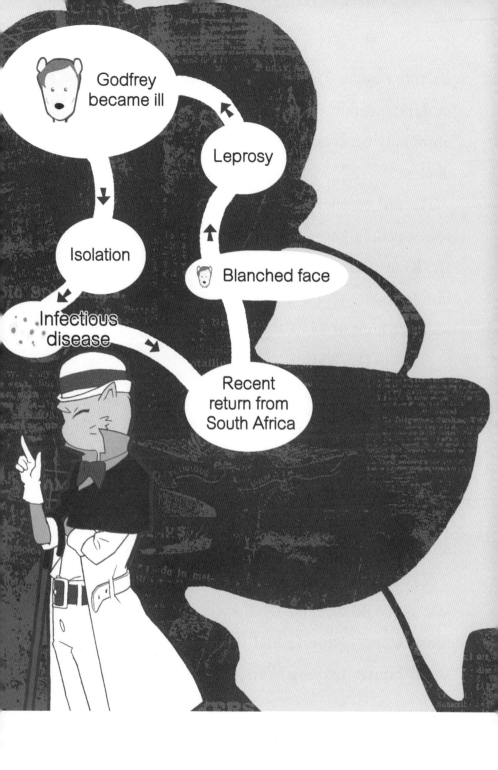

doctors besides Dr. Kent?" asked Holmes. "You must understand that this is a very serious disease. It is absolutely necessary to get a second opinion from other doctors."

The old colonel shook his head and said, "No. The fewer people know about Godfrey's illness, the better. Dr. Kent is the only doctor in this town. I've known him for many years. I would only trust him to keep the secret to himself."

"This is Dr. Watson. He is a highly skilled medical doctor. He also has considerable knowledge in the subject of leprosy. Would you mind if he examines Godfrey?" suggested Holmes.

The old colonel nodded in agreement. He was not expecting any miracles, but he also had no reason to refuse a second opinion.

"Let's step outside and give them more room, so Dr. Watson could examine Godfrey in detail." After saying those words, Holmes and the others went out of the small house, leaving Watson and Godfrey inside by themselves.

Harp's Cane

Holmes, Colonel Emsworth, Dodd and Ralph all waited with heavy hearts outside the small wooden house. Everyone was quiet. Deep down they all knew that the chances of Watson announcing miraculous good news was slim to none.

After a few minutes, the black dog named Rocky that was lying quietly on the ground suddenly jumped to its feet, staring at the direction of the front gate in alert. The men found the dog's behaviour rather odd, so they all looked towards the front gate as well. The group could see two men from afar. These two men were none other than our familiar Gorilla and Fox. Perhaps their work in the woods was finished and now they had made their way to the estate.

Fox noticed there were people on the far lawn, so he raised the cane in his hand and waved it at the group.

miraculous (形) 奇蹟般的

"Woof, woof, woof, woof!" barked Rocky all of a sudden as it charged wildly towards Gorilla and Fox.

Seeing a ferocious dog dashing towards them, Gorilla and Fox let out a frightened yelp and ran for their lives. For some reason, Rocky totally ignored Gorilla and focused **strictly** on Fox in a mad chase.

"This black dog certainly knows how to pick its prey, choosing to hunt after the smaller, weaker target," said Holmes lightly as he watched Fox run in **frantic** circles. This comedic scene playing before the group lifted the sad and heavy mood surrounding them just a minute ago.

"Aarrgghh! Help! Someone, please help me!" Fox kept running as fast as he could, but Rocky seemed determined to keep chasing until he was able to bite a piece off Fox.

"Use the cane to hit him, you **daft** fool!"

strictly (副) 僅僅、完全地　　frantic (形) 發狂般的　　daft (形) 愚笨的

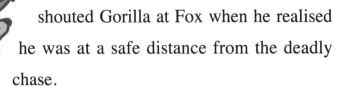

shouted Gorilla at Fox when he realised
he was at a safe distance from the deadly
chase.

Only after hearing Gorilla's
shouts did Fox remember he was holding
a weapon in his hand. Fox quickly
turned around and tried to strike
the cane at Rocky, but Rocky was
even quicker than Fox, dodging the
strike with a swift *twist* of its body. Fox was so terrified
that he began to *wield* the cane wildly at the dog like
a mad man, but each swing only struck air and none
landed on Rocky.

When Fox slowed down for a second to catch his
breath, Rocky *seized* the opportunity to lunge at Fox.
Curiously enough, Rocky did not bite
Fox at all; its jaws *clenched*
right onto the cane instead.

"You bad dog! Don't
you dare take away my

twist (動) 扭動　wield (動) 揮動　seize(d) (動) 利用、抓住
clench(ed) (動) 緊緊咬着

weapon!" shouted Fox angrily at Rocky, refusing to let go of the cane. The deadly chase had now turned into a tug of war, but the dog was much stronger than the man. One swift jerk from the dog and Fox instantly lost his grip on the cane.

"You daft fool! Don't let the dog take away our material evidence!" yelled Gorilla.

"What material evidence?" Holmes ran over to Gorilla and asked, "Are you saying that cane is material evidence?"

"Why are you here? Have you come here to look for Harp too?" Gorilla was too busy dealing with the fierce black dog earlier that he did not notice Holmes was also on the estate until now.

"I'll tell you later. Please answer my question first," said Holmes impatiently.

Fox had also run over to

tug of war (名) 拔河比賽

Holmes at this time. In between catching his breath, he said to Holmes, "That is Harp's cane. Someone had sent it to Harp's secretary, asking her to bring along the cane and meet in the woods if she wanted to know the whereabouts of Harp."

"Harp's secretary was afraid that this meeting might be risky and dangerous, so she came to us for help," added Gorilla. "We went to the woods earlier, following the map that was drawn by the sender, but we didn't see anyone in the woods. Now we're here to see Colonel Emsworth. According to Harp's secretary, the last thing Harp told her before he went missing was that he had come here to investigate..."

"Woof, woof, woof!" Rocky's barks cut off Gorilla in mid-sentence. Turning his head towards the direction of the barks, Holmes could see Rocky approaching them with the cane between its jaws. The dog ran to Ralph then dropped the cane on the ground in front of its master while wagging its tail with all its might.

Watching the interaction between the dog and its owner, Holmes let out a shrewd chuckle and said, "Perhaps we will be able to locate Harp very soon."

Both Gorilla and Fox were deeply confused. They did not understand what our great detective meant by that utterance.

Holmes walked over to Ralph and said, "Please tell us where is that private detective named Harp."

shrewd (形) 狡猾的   utterance (名) 說話、言論

From the look in Ralph's eyes, Holmes's sudden inquiry had clearly thrown Ralph into a slight panic, but Ralph quickly gathered his _composure_ and said to Holmes, "I'm sorry, but I don't know what you are talking about. Who is Harp?"

"Please drop the _pretence_!" Holmes pointed at the cane on the ground and said, "That cane belongs to Harp. Your dog chased after the cane as soon as it saw

the cane, which meant it had seen Harp and the cane before. Your dog brought the cane to you then wagged

composure (名) 鎮靜、沉着   pretence (名) 裝模作樣

its tail and waited for its reward, which meant you had also seen Harp before, and probably did something horrible to Harp too!"

"I don't understand what you mean. I don't know any man named Harp," denied Ralph fervently but his eyes were shifting unsteadily. Ralph was obviously guilty of something.

"What is going on? What are you talking about?" asked the oblivious old colonel.

Right at that moment, Watson and Godfrey stepped out of the small house. The group's attention quickly switched over to them.

oblivious (形) 蒙在鼓裏的

Watson walked towards the old colonel with a gentle smile on his face and said, "Usually, under these circumstances, I would be bringing bad news to the patient's family. But this time is different. I have good news for you, sir. What Godfrey has is **ichthyosis** , not leprosy. **Symptoms** of both conditions are similar, which is why **diagnosis** could often be mixed up sometimes."

ichthyosis (名) 魚鱗癬　　symptom(s) (名) 症狀　　diagnosis (名) 診斷

"Really?" Colonel Emsworth, Dodd and Ralph were all pleasantly surprised. They could not believe their ears and were stunned speechless. Dodd was the first to shift his reaction from shock to joy. He leapt towards Godfrey at once and gave his best mate a hearty bear bug.

Everyone was moved by Dodd and Godfrey's long-awaited, happy reunion.

However, a terrifying cry also sounded from the group all of a sudden.

"Oh no…! Oh no…!"

As though the cries were coming from the depths of hell, the hoarse voice uttering the cries was filled with immense guilt and sorrow.

"What is it, Ralph? Are you alright?" Godfrey was taken aback from the old butler's sudden lamenting cries.

"Harp… His name was Harp? We're so stupid. Young master Godfrey is not a leper… We killed him for no reason… We killed an innocent man…" muttered Ralph as he recounted the happenings of that night.

lamenting (形) 悲痛的

114

That day was the 6th of February. A man from London checked into a hotel near the local train station. The man went to ask the hotel's owner, Juniper, for information on Godfrey and the colonel's home. Juniper found the man **suspicious**, so he went to his good friend Gordon to discuss the matter. Gordon was a pub owner, and it turned out the man had also gone into his pub and asked many questions before checking into the hotel. So both Juniper and Gordon were pretty sure that the man was a private detective.

With a bad feeling about this visitor, Juniper and Gordon came to me to discuss how we should handle the situation. Those two already knew about young master Godfrey's unfortunate infection of leprosy. In a small town like this, no secrets could be kept for long. Everyone in this town knows about Godfrey's illness, but we have all made a **tacit pact** to keep this secret to ourselves and not utter a word to outsiders, because everyone has great respect for the colonel. We are all **indebted** to his immense generosity one way or another.

There is also another reason why we do not wish

suspicious (形) 可疑的　tacit pact (名) 默契
indebted (形) 受過恩惠的、感激的

for this secret to be exposed. As you probably already know, this small town's economy is mainly supported by tourism. Many visitors come here during hunting season between summer and autumn. If word spreads out that there is a leper in town, people would feel reluctant to come here for holiday. Businesses like hotels and pubs that mainly rely on tourists would be hit hard.

That's why Juniper and Gordon were so concerned. Needless to say, the one person who dreaded the most about this secret leaking out was I. I must protect the reputation of the Emsworth household, and I certainly do not want the young master to get hurt. He is already suffering enough from an unfortunate illness. So we persuaded Dr. Kent to join us to keep an eye on the private detective.

Just as we had expected, that private detective stepped out of the hotel after the night had fallen and walked along the road towards the estate. But when he reached the woods, he seemed to have noticed that he was being followed since he suddenly turned around to leave. To deter him from coming back, I unleashed Rocky to scare him. Who knew that he would start beating Rocky with

reluctant (形) 不願意的   dread(ed) (動) 害怕、擔心   reputation (名) 名譽
deter (動) 阻撓、阻止   unleash(ed) (動) 解開

116

his cane? He did not manage to strike a blow at Rocky though, so he *tossed* his cane at Rocky instead then fled into the woods. That's how he fell into an abandoned well by accident.

He was not moving at all when we found him at the bottom of the well. We thought that he must have died from the fall, so we decided to cover the well with a **hefty lid** and stow away the body for good. I knew that if someone were to find his body, the police would come here and conduct a thorough investigation, upon which Godfrey's illness would be exposed to the world. With

the well sealed, I was hoping that the secret of the young master's condition would also be sealed forever.

toss(ed) (動) 拋　abandoned (形) 荒廢的　hefty lid (形＋名) 沉重的蓋子
stow away (片語動) 藏起來

The Secret
at the Bottom of the Well

"How could you have done that? What if that private detective weren't dead? That would be murder!" shouted Godfrey angrily after listening to Ralph's recount of the incident.

"I'm so sorry, but that didn't cross my mind at the time. No one objected the idea, so we just..." said the old butler as he lowered his head in immense guilt.

"Where is that abandoned well? Take us there right now," said Holmes to Ralph.

"Yes! Lead the way quickly!" urged Gorilla and Fox.

Ralph nodded and led everyone into the woods. It did not take long for the group to reach the abandoned well. The hefty lid was still lying heavily on top of the well, just like it was on the night of the incident.

Everyone stood around the well as though they were

observing a moment of silence. With his eyes tightly shut and his legs trembling uncontrollably, Ralph was too afraid to bear witness to the crime that he had "buried" with his own hands.

Drawing a deep breath, Holmes bent down and gripped the edge of the hefty lid then said to Gorilla and Fox, "Let's remove this lid."

The Scotland Yard duo nodded their heads then gripped firmly onto the edge of the lid.

"One, two, three!" On the count of three, they removed the hefty lid then leaned over to look down the well. However, the three men all gasped in shock after just one look.

Is it really that scary? These three men are seasoned *investigators who have seen it all. Is the condition of this* decaying *corpse so horrible that even these three are shocked to the bone?* thought Watson sceptically

seasoned (形) 老練的、經驗豐富的　　decaying (形) 腐化的、腐爛的
corpse (名) 屍體

119

before he leaned forward to look down the well himself.

"How could this be? Where is the body?" cried the astonished Watson.

Taken aback by Watson's words, Colonel Emsworth, Dodd and Godfrey also leaned forward to look down the well. Sure enough, the bottom of the dried-up well was clearly empty!

"How could this be? Are you sure you really did see Harp at the bottom of the well?" shouted Gorilla as he pulled Ralph by the lapel .

"Yes…yes… Is his body not at the bottom of the well? But I saw the body with my own eyes," said Ralph in a low, quivering voice.

"Is it possible that he had only fainted from the fall? Then upon waking up, he climbed out of the well by himself?" asked Dodd in a mutter.

"I don't think so," said Holmes bluntly. "If he were able to climb out of the well by himself, he would've returned to London already. He wouldn't still be missing."

lapel (名) 衣領　　quivering (形) 抖顫的　　bluntly (副) 單刀直入地、直言不諱

"Then... Someone must've moved the body," said Watson.

"That's the only possibility," nodded Holmes. "But who moved the body?"

All of a sudden, Rocky ran off to a far spot in the woods. "Woof, woof, woof, woof!" barked Rocky to the group from a distance.

"Perhaps the clever dog has found the answer for us," said Holmes as he ran towards Rocky, then the others also *followed suit*.

With Rocky leading them into the deep forest, the group ran for more than ten minutes before a log cabin finally came to sight.

"That is a log cabin for hunters. Nobody comes here for hunting during winter so it should be empty," said the old colonel.

Rocky was the first to reach the log cabin, barking as loud as it could to indicate the location to the group. All of a sudden, the cabin's front door opened and out came a short gentleman, seemingly startled by the loud barks,

follow(ed) suit (習) 跟着做

but he was even more taken aback when he saw the group of men approaching the cabin.

The old colonel and Godfrey stepped towards the short gentleman and asked, "Dr. Kent, what are you doing here?"

"I…" Perhaps he was too surprised by the unexpected visit, Kent looked over to Ralph then to Dodd and the rest of group, apparently lost for words.

Gorilla leapt forward at once and confronted the doctor in a harsh tone, "Is your name Kent? Did you move Harp's dead body?"

"What dead body? I didn't move any dead body," said Kent as he shook his head frantically.

"Stop acting daft! Did you destroy the dead body and *scrub* away all the evidence?" Refusing to be **outdone** by Gorilla, Fox also joined in the **interrogation** with his roaring shouts.

"Destroy the dead body? I did no such thing, honest

scrub (動) 洗擦　　outdo(ne) (動) 勝過、先聲奪人
interrogation (名) 審問

to God!" denied Kent.

"You **outrageous creep**! Ralph has confessed to his involvement already. You can't deny your way out of this!" shouted Gorilla furiously.

"No. He is telling the truth," said Holmes who was standing by the front door of the log cabin and pointing his thumb towards the interior. "Harp is inside. He is not dead."

Before anyone had time to react to Holmes's surprising announcement, a middle-aged man was already limping his way out of the front door with a **crutch** in his hand. Needless to say, this limping

outrageous (形) 無恥的、可惡的   creep (名) 討厭鬼
limp(ing) (動) 瘸着腳走、跛行   crutch (名) 枴杖

man was the private detective named Harp who had been missing in the past few days.

As soon as he saw Harp, Ralph lost all strength in his legs and fell to the ground on his knees. Tears streamed down Ralph's face as he **wailed plaintively**, his cries *tugging at* **heartstrings**. The group all knew that those were cries of both sorrow and relief. Ralph was deeply sorry that he had almost committed a *monstrous* crime, but he was also relieved to see Harp had survived the terrible ordeal.

Once they were all at the police station, Kent told his side of the story on what happened that night. After Kent, Ralph, Juniper and Gordon placed the hefty lid on the well, they all left the woods and went home. However, Kent went back to the well shortly

wail(ed) (動) 放聲大哭　plaintively (副) 悲傷地
tug(ging) at heartstrings (習) 觸動心弦　monstrous (形) 可怕的

afterwards to check whether Harp was really dead or not, because if Harp were not dead, then sealing Harp in the well would be the same as killing Harp. The four of them would become murderers committing the most unforgiveable sin of all. Sure enough, when Kent went back to the well, he could hear some weak coughs coming from inside the well. It turned out that Harp had only broken his leg from the fall and was still alive.

Kent pulled Harp out from the dried-up well, but he did not dare to send Harp to the hospital. He was afraid that his **accomplices** might really plan to kill Harp if they were to find out Harp was still alive. So Kent decided to hide Harp away in a remote log cabin where hardly anyone ever passed by. While treating Harp's injuries, Kent negotiated with Harp, hoping that Harp would keep quiet about everything when Harp was well enough to return home. Harp had no reason to refuse his rescuer's request. As soon as Harp's recovery was strong enough to walk with a crutch, Kent sent Harp's cane along with a letter to Harp's secretary, hoping that she would come and help take Harp home. However,

accomplice(s) (名) 同黨

coming to meet Kent in the woods were two suspicious-looking men instead of Harp's secretary. Needless to say, those two suspicious-looking men were Gorilla and Fox. Unsure of their identities and intentions, Kent decided not to come out and meet those two men.

After the whole story had finally come to light, Holmes and Watson boarded the next train back to London while Gorilla and Fox stayed behind to handle the leftover affairs concerning Ralph and the others.

"What a bizarre case," said the intrigued Watson after finding their seats on the train.

"Bizarre indeed. It's most fortunate that both Harp and Godfrey are fine, otherwise it could've been a terrible tragedy." Holmes let out a deep sigh before continuing, "In a way, there weren't any real villains in this case. The old butler Ralph, Dr. Kent, the hotel owner and the pub owner were all simple, decent people. Murder was an idea that never crossed their minds. It just so happened that they were forced into a situation that made them think they had no other choice."

"That is true. If Harp hadn't fallen down the well, I

bizarre (形) 奇異古怪的、怪誕的　　intrigued (形) 好奇的

don't think they would have the guts to kill a man **with their bare hands**," agreed Watson.

Looking pensively at the scenery passing by the train window, Holmes nodded and said, "That just shows how fragile human nature can be. When placed in a specific situation under certain circumstances, even those who never step **out of bounds**, those who would never willingly harm anyone, not even an ant, could lose their conscience and commit the most heinous sins in a flash. That's why we should always stay alert and be mindful at all times."

---

with one's bare hands (片語) 赤手空拳、徒手　　pensively (副) 沉思地、若有所思地
fragile (形) 脆弱的　　out of bounds (片語) 越界　　conscience (名) 良知
mindful (形) 小心的、留心的

Missing ①

Why are you looking so glum?

I didn't have a part to play this time. It's not fair.

This case happened out of town. There's nothing I could do.

But I'm a main character. I should appear in the story all the time.

I've figured out a way.

Really? What is it?

I can say in the story that you've gone missing. This way you will play a part without needing to appear at all!

Missing ②

I want to fake a missing person case to scare Mr. Holmes.

That sounds fun! Let me help you.

Really?

Mr. Holmes, Bunny has gone missing!

Should we call the police?

Why should we call the police?

How frustrating!

......

Let's savour the peace and silence instead.

128

Being trapped inside a well sounds so scary.

You feel scared?

What are you doing?

I'm heading out to practise running. I'm joining the marathon tomorrow.

Of course! I would starve to death!

I don't think so.

But you don't practice regularly. Starting your practise now is the same as digging a well when you feel thirsty. It's useless.

You shouldn't say that!

You are ignorant yet full of yourself…

I'm only telling you for your own good.

You basically live your life like a frog in a well, but I don't see you starving to death.

Haven't you heard of the Chinese proverb "river water does not interfere with well water"? You should mind your own business!

river water

well water

Sherlock Holmes Cool Science Magic Trick
The Coin Has Gone Missing!

The missing cases this time are very bizarre.

I also know a little r trick that could mal something disappea Do you want to see

1

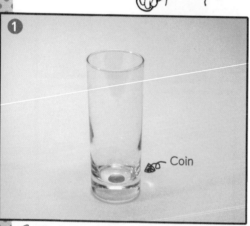

Coin

 Find a tall glass and place a coin underneath the glass.

2

Coin

 Pour some water into the glass and the coi would appear to be rising with the water le

3

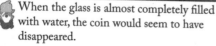 When the glass is almost completely filled with water, the coin would seem to have disappeared.

Unfolding the Scientific Myster

Actually, the coin has not gone missing at all. You will find the coin still at the same spot if you remove the gla In this little magic trick, the audience is fooled by light refraction. When the glass is empty, light rays shine in a straight line through the glass and onto the coin. At the same time, light rays are also reflected in a straight line from the coin to our eyes. This is why we can clearl see the coin under the glass. But when water is poured into the glass, light rays passing through the water are refracted. The refracted light rays rise with the water lev making the coin appear to be rising until it disappears. This is a very neat trick, but if the glass is not tall enough, the coin might appear to be floating on the water surface instead of gone missing even when water is filled to the rim of the glass, which is also a very interesting sight.

THE GREAT DETECTIVE SHERLOCK HOLMES

—— THE BLANCHED SOLDIER —— ⑱

Original Story – Sir Arthur Conan Doyle
(This book is adapted from the story *The Blanched Soldier.*)

Adapter and Producer – Lai Ho

English Translator – Maria Kan

English Editor – Monica Leong

Illustrator – Yu Yuen Wong

Annotator – Lynn Hall

Cover Design – Chan Yuk Lung, Yip Shing Chi

Content Design – Mak Kwok Lung

Editors – Chan Ping Kwan, Kwok Tin Bo, So Wai Yee, Wong Suk Yee

First published in Hong Kong in 2023 by
Rightman Publishing Limited
2A, Cheung Lee Industrial Building, 9 Cheung Lee Street, Chai Wan, Hong Kong

Text : © Lui Hok Cheung
Copyright © 2023 by Rightman Publishing Ltd. All rights reserved.

Printed and bound by
Rainbow Printings Limited
3-4 Floor, 26-28 Tai Yau Street, San Po Kong, Kowloon, Hong Kong

Distributed by
Tung Tak Newspaper & Magazine Agency Co., Ltd.
Ground Floor, Yeung Yiu Chung No.5 Industrial Building, 34 Tai Yip Street, Kwun Tong, Kowloon, Hong Kong
Tel: (852) 3551-3388   Fax: (852) 3551- 3300

ISBN:978-988-8504-60-2
HK$68 / NT$340

If damages or missing pages of the book are found, please contact us by calling (852) 2515-8787.

The latest news on
The Great Detective Sherlock Holmes
or if you have any thoughts and comments,
please visit our Facebook page at
www.facebook.com/great.holmes

大偵探福爾摩斯

Online purchasing is easy and convenient.
Free delivery in Hong Kong for one purchase above HK$100.
For details, please visit www.rightman.net.